DANCE DIVAS

On Pointe

DANCE DIVAS

Showtime!

Two to Tango

Let's Rock!

Step It Up

On Pointe

Showstopper
(coming soon)

DANCE DIVAS
On Pointe

Sheryl Berk

BLOOMSBURY
NEW YORK   LONDON   NEW DELHI   SYDNEY

First published in the United States of America in December 2014
by Bloomsbury Children's Books
www.bloomsbury.com

Bloomsbury is a registered trademark of Bloomsbury Publishing Plc

For information about permission to reproduce selections from this book, write to
Permissions, Bloomsbury Children's Books, 1385 Broadway, New York, New York 10018
Bloomsbury books may be purchased for business or promotional use. For information on
bulk purchases please contact Macmillan Corporate and Premium Sales Department at
specialmarkets@macmillan.com

Library of Congress Cataloging-in-Publication Data
Berk, Sheryl.
On pointe / by Sheryl Berk.
pages   cm   — (Dance Divas)
Summary: Anya, Liberty, and Scarlett all think they'll be a shoo-in for the lead role
of Clara in Dances Minnelli's annual production of *The Nutcracker*, but Gracie gets
the part—and the pressure—while the others must be content with supporting roles.
ISBN 978-1-61963-586-9 (paperback) • ISBN 978-1-61963-585-2 (hardcover)
ISBN 978-1-61963-587-6 (e-book)
[1. Ballet dancing—Fiction. 2. Dance—Fiction. 3. Interpersonal relations—Fiction.
4. Dance teams—Fiction. 5. Nutcracker (Choreographic work)—Fiction.] I. Title.
PZ7.B45236On 2014   [Fic]—dc23   2014022842

Book design by Donna Mark
Typeset by Westchester Book Composition
Printed and bound in the U.S.A. by Thomson-Shore Inc., Dexter, Michigan
2 4 6 8 10 9 7 5 3 (paperback)
2 4 6 8 10 9 7 5 3 1 (hardcover)

*To Francis Patrelle and everyone at dP and
The Yorkville Nutcracker. Thank you for your
dedication, inspiration, and perspiration, and
for making magic onstage year after year!*

Table of Contents

1 Going Nuts   1
2 Casting Call   9
3 And 5, 6, 7, 8 ...   19
4 Tiny Dancer   26
5 That's the Way the Cookie Crumbles   39
6 New Boy on the Block   45
7 Spaced Out   56
8 Birthday Blastoff   64
9 Get to the Pointe   68
10 Scene and Heard   73
11 Diva in Training   85
12 A Brewing Storm   92
13 Snow Business   101
14 We're All in This Together   111
15 Curtains Up   116
16 Home Sweet Home   124
   Glossary of Dance Terms   129
   Acknowledgments   131

DANCE DIVAS
On Pointe

CHAPTER 1

Going Nuts

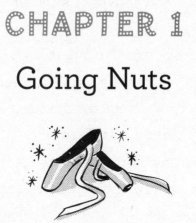

Anya Bazarov walked past the bulletin board outside Dance Divas studio 1 and did a double take. She yanked a flyer down and raced into the dressing room, where the rest of her teammates were getting ready for ballet class.

"Did you see this?" she asked excitedly, waving the sheet of paper in the air.

"I can't see it unless you stand still," replied Liberty. She stood up and grabbed the paper out of Anya's hand and read aloud: "'Dances Minnelli presents *A New Jersey Nutcracker*.' Yeah? So?"

"So? So keep reading. They're casting it next

weekend! They're looking for dancers to play the leads!" Anya said.

"Lemme see that," Scarlett said. "I've always dreamed of playing Clara in *The Nutcracker*."

"I've always wanted to be the Sugar Plum Fairy," Anya said. "Since I was seven years old and saw it for the first time at the Los Angeles Ballet."

Scarlett read the details on the flyer. " 'Wanted: children ages seven to sixteen for principal roles. Must have at least two years of dance experience and be currently enrolled in a preprofessional dance program.' "

"Do you think they'll have the Land of Sweets scene?" Bria asked. "I'd love to be one of the Spanish hot chocolate dancers. Or the Arabian coffee!"

"And I could be one of the Russian candy canes," Rochelle said. "They have the best music and the coolest moves."

Scarlett's little sister, Gracie, had been barely paying attention. But the word "sweets" suddenly piqued her interest. "What do you mean 'Land of Sweets'?" she asked.

"Oh, it's so beautiful!" Anya explained. "Clara and the prince travel to a breathtaking candy land where candies from all over the world perform for them. And the Sugar Plum Fairy is in charge!"

"Don't you remember Gram taking us to see *The Nutcracker* at Lincoln Center in New York City a few years ago?" Scarlett asked her. "You were about four years old and all you wanted to do was go home. You kept ducking under the seat when the Mouse King came onstage."

Gracie shrugged. "I kinda remember the creepy mouse guy. Oh! And Grandma buying us hot dogs from a cart on the street outside the theater."

Scarlett rolled her eyes. "Of course all you'd remember about this gorgeous ballet is what you ate, Gracie."

Gracie pouted. "Well, I'm older now. I'm seven and three-quarters, and the paper says you need to be seven to audition. I wanna be in the show, too."

"I can totally see you as one of the cute and fuzzy little mice," Anya teased her. She got down on all fours and pretended to sniff around the dressing room floor. "Squeak! Squeak!"

"Those mice were not cute and fuzzy!" Gracie protested. "They were gray and ugly with long tails and twitchy noses. I am not playing a mean mouse."

"I think Gracie has reindeer written all over her," Bria suggested. "You know? One of the little guys who pull Clara's sleigh?"

"Reindeer are okay," Gracie said. "At least they're cute and they don't scare people. What other parts are there?"

Anya did a graceful *pirouette*. "There's also the beautiful Snow Queen—or Dew Drop Fairy, who dances the 'Waltz of the Flowers,'" she said.

"Clara is the best part," Scarlett added. "She's the main character and she gets to do a gorgeous *pas de deux* with the Nutcracker Prince."

"Ooh! I wanna be Clara!" Gracie said, clapping her hands together excitedly. "Especially if she gets to dance with a prince and go to Candyland!"

Liberty chuckled. "Dream on, Gracie. I'm sure they'll cast someone with infinitely more ballet talent and experience. That would be me."

"Excuse me?" Anya jumped in. "Or me."

"Or me!" Scarlett said.

"Just a second. I know *all* about *The Nutcracker*," Bria said. "Not only have I seen it every year since I was three years old with my family, but I know the whole history. I did a term paper on it. It was adapted from E. T. A. Hoffmann's story *The Nutcracker and the Mouse King*, and it premiered in 1892 in St. Petersburg. Tchaikovsky wrote the score."

"Bria, you are a human Google search engine." Scarlett chuckled.

"Maybe for dance. Just not for biology or pre-algebra," Bria said. "My brain crashes on those subjects."

"You'd crash and burn as Clara, too," Liberty said. "There's no way you'll beat me for that part."

"Maybe Hayden and I will be Clara and her prince," Rochelle added. She and her "boyfriend" had always wanted to perform together again, and this was the perfect opportunity.

"Don't make me laugh," Liberty snickered. "You? Clara? *Puh-lease!* But Hayden and I would certainly make a great team again. Did you forget when we won best duet at Leaps and Bounds?"

Rochelle gritted her teeth. How could she forget? If she hadn't sprained her ankle, the trophy—and the duet with Hayden—would have been hers.

"That's all very nice," Anya said, piping up. "But I'm the one with the most ballet training."

"Says who?" Liberty stared her down. "It's not what you know in this biz, it's *who* you know. And I bet my mom knows the choreographer for Dances Minnelli."

"There you go again," Rochelle said. "Always running to your Hollywood choreographer mommy to call in special favors."

Scarlett stepped in to referee. "Divas, Divas! Aren't we getting a little ahead of ourselves here? The audition is next week. We'll just all have to prepare and practice and see how it goes. Plus, we need to ask Miss Toni's permission."

With several competitions coming up, she wasn't sure how their dance coach would feel about them taking time off to rehearse and do a different show.

The dressing room suddenly became silent, as each of the girls began to formulate her game plan for winning the lead. Rochelle was texting Hayden; Liberty went off to call her mom; Anya did another *pirouette*; and Scarlett and Gracie gathered around Bria's laptop to see what other information they could find out about the production.

"It says here that 'Dances Minnelli's *New Jersey Nutcracker* will be the only *Nutcracker* in the tristate area to feature an all-kid cast,'" Bria read. "Even the adults in the opening party scene will be played by kids."

"What else does it say?" Scarlett asked. "Any hints as to what they're looking for in a Clara? Like, oh, maybe a redhead?" She twirled a long, curly strand of hair around her fingertips.

Bria scanned the website. "Nope, just lots of stuff on how the setting is really unique and non-traditional. The set for the Land of Sweets will look just like the boardwalk in Wildwood, New Jersey, complete with a working Ferris wheel onstage."

"Cool!" Gracie squealed. "I hope Miss Toni lets us do the show."

Bria's face went white. "Um, I'm not so sure she will. Take a look at this." She pointed to a line of fine print. "Directed by Marcus Sanzobar."

"Oh my gosh! As in Toni's ex? The guy who broke her heart when she was a student at American Ballet Company?" Scarlett exclaimed. "The guy who dumped her for Justine Chase, coach of City Feet?"

Bria nodded. "How many professional ballet dancers named Marcus Sanzobar could there be? Maybe we should leave that part out when we ask her . . ."

CHAPTER 2
Casting Call

Miss Toni demanded several things from her elite dance team: cooperation, coordination, and perspiration. But perhaps the most important thing was punctuality. If the clock ticked a second past the scheduled class time, it set even her teeth on edge.

"You're late!" she barked as Scarlett, Bria, Anya, and Gracie raced through the ballet studio door at 5:02 p.m. "Class starts at five p.m. sharp. Where are the rest?"

Liberty and Rochelle practically knocked each other over to get through the door at the same time.

"Here!" Liberty shouted. "I would have been here sooner, but my mom had to put me on hold. Rihanna was on the other line."

Rochelle muttered under her breath, "Name dropper," then took her spot at the *barre* next to Scarlett. "I think you should ask Toni about *The Nutcracker*," she told her friend.

"Me? Why me?" Scarlett whispered. She hated the idea of having to break the news to her teacher that Marcus was back on the dance scene.

"She likes you—and you're our fearless leader," Rochelle said, giving her a shove forward. "Go on!"

Scarlett took a deep breath. "Miss Toni, uh, we were just wondering . . ."

"I was wondering, too," Toni said, interrupting. "I was wondering why we are wasting so much time today instead of beginning our ballet exercises at the *barre*. How can any of you expect to be real dancers one day if you don't put in the work now?"

All the girls gulped as they prepared for one of Miss Toni's famous lectures.

"And how are any of you going to get a principal role in *A New Jersey Nutcracker* if you don't practice?" she continued.

Anya gasped. "But—but how did you know?"

Toni smiled. "Who do you think put up that flyer on the bulletin board? I expect my Divas to represent our studio at that audition in a week and take every one of those lead roles."

Rochelle groaned. It was just like Toni to turn any situation—even a lovely holiday ballet—into a competition. "So you're cool with us doing it? Even if it means we'll be busy with rehearsals and performances?"

"You will make up every single class you miss here at Dance Divas," she said. "Being in *The Nutcracker* is a bonus for you. Icing on the cake."

"Sounds like tons more work to me," Bria whispered. "And I'm barely able to keep up with my homework as it is!"

"The ballet's performances are over the holiday break, so we won't have any competitions until after the new year," Toni said. "I think it's an excellent way to keep you on your toes when you're out of my sight."

Anya's hand went up. "But what if we don't get cast?"

Toni's smile faded. "*That*," she said, and paused to look at each of the girls before continuing, "is not an option."

* * *

The Divas were used to seeing tons of dancers at competitions almost every weekend, but never this many people in one place. The rehearsal space at Dances Minnelli was packed with kids of all ages who all wanted the same thing.

"My name is Amanda and I want to play Clara," said a short girl with dark brown hair scooped into a high ponytail. She wore a crop top that read DANCE, SLEEP, REPEAT and leopard-print leggings. She gave all her information to Miss Andrea, the polite young woman taking the applications one by one.

"And where do you dance?" Miss Andrea smiled sweetly.

"Carrie B's School of Hip-Hop," Amanda replied proudly.

The woman rested her glasses on the tip of her nose. "No, I mean ballet, dear."

"I don't really take ballet lessons, so to speak," Amanda replied. "But I am really flexible!" She dropped and did a handstand—on one hand.

"Hmm, okay. Make your way into studio two for ages ten and up."

"This is ridiculous," Liberty said, adjusting a bobby pin in her bun. "Am I the only qualified dancer here?"

Hayden elbowed Rochelle. "Promise me you won't hurt yourself again and leave me dancing with her." He pointed to Liberty.

"Promise!" Rochelle smiled, squeezing his hand. "We're a shoo-in for Clara and the prince."

"Think again," Liberty replied. "A friend of a friend of my mom's called and spoke to Mr. Minnelli himself. He can't wait to cast me."

"Cast you as what?" Rochelle fired back. "I doubt there's a costume large enough to fit your big head."

Hayden stepped between them. "Girls, play nice."

"Hayden's right," Scarlett said, backing him up. "We promised Miss Toni we'd be on our best behavior."

Rochelle shrugged. "She started it."

Miss Andrea handed each girl a number to pin on their leotards.

"I'm number seventy-five. How about you?" Anya asked Scarlett.

"Number one hundred seventeen. This is crazy! How many hundreds of people are auditioning?"

"Speak for yourself," Liberty said, flexing her feet in her toe shoes. "A little competition never scares me."

"There's competition, and there's *competition*," Bria said. "I'm number two hundred eighty-one. I'm not even sure I'll get to audition at all today."

Just then, a dapper-looking man with graying hair and a pink bow tie pushed between the rows of dancers. "Pardon me, coming through," he said, waving a walking stick in the air.

Gracie smiled. "That's a really cool stick," she said, admiring the silver-tipped handle.

The man stopped in his tracks. "You think so?" he asked her. "Well, you have extremely good taste. Her Highness herself gave it to me."

"The queen of England?" Gracie asked. "Did you meet her?"

"I was referring to the great Cynthia Gregory, America's *prima ballerina assoluta*. She gifted it to me when I choreographed her at San Francisco Ballet."

"Oh." Gracie giggled. "Does she have a crown? 'Cause if not, I could make her one with some cardboard and tin foil. If my mom would let me. Last weekend she said my art projects make too much of a mess."

The man's eyes grew wide. "You're quite a gabber aren't you, little girl?"

"What's a gabber?" Gracie replied. "It's not something mean is it? Because my sister, Scoot, always says if you don't have something nice to say, you shouldn't say anything at all."

"Gracie!" Scarlett said, covering her mouth with her hand. "I'm so sorry, sir. Whenever Gracie gets nervous, she can't stop talking."

Gracie wiggled free of her grasp. "I'm not nervous! I'm going to get the part of Clara and eat all the candy I want," she declared proudly.

"Is that so?" the man asked. "We shall see." Then he winked and continued toward the dance studio at the end of the hallway.

"Who was that?" Rochelle asked.

Bria held up her phone. "*That* was Mr. Minnelli. See—his picture is on the Dances Minnelli website."

"Gracie," Scarlett scolded her. "Why did you bother him? You may have just blown all of our chances to get a lead!"

"I did not," Gracie insisted. "He was the one who said I was a grabber."

"A gabber, not a grabber," Scarlett corrected her. "Honestly, if you can't act like a big girl, you don't belong here auditioning."

Gracie crossed her arms over her chest. "I *am*

a big girl. I'm almost eight. So there!" She marched ahead of Scarlett to where Miss Andrea was lining up the younger dancers. As she walked into the studio, she stuck her tongue out at her big sister.

"She drives me nuts!" Scarlett sighed, leaning on Rochelle's shoulder. Her toe shoes were pinching from standing in them for so long.

"Don't you mean she drives you nutcrackers?" Rochelle teased her.

"I don't know how you guys can joke around at a time like this," Anya said. She had already stretched several times and was now doing deep *pliés* against the wall. "Aren't you nervous?"

"I don't get nervous," Liberty bragged.

But Anya noticed that Liberty was drumming her foot on the floor.

Miss Andrea stood on a chair and clapped her hands to get everyone's attention. "May I please have numbers one through one hundred in studio one; one hundred one through two hundred in studio two; and two hundred one through three hundred in studio three," she shouted over the noise. "Does everyone know where they're supposed to be?"

Liberty and Anya headed for the first door while Scarlett, Rochelle, and Hayden went to the second. Bria was the only one of the Divas in the third group.

"Break a leg!" she called after them.

CHAPTER 3

And 5, 6, 7, 8 . . .

The youngest dancers were all seated on the floor of studio four when Miss Andrea and Mr. Minnelli walked in. The ballet mistress, Miss Noreen, was taking attendance.

"I need Olivia, Julia, Alexa, Madison, and Gracie over here," she said, pointing to the center of the floor. "Please stand in first position."

The girls all stood up and took a spot in front of the mirrors. Gracie skipped over and waved to Mr. Minnelli.

"I'm going to teach you a little combination," Miss Noreen explained. "Everyone watch, because you'll have to do it, too," she instructed the other children gathered on both sides of the room.

The routine was fairly simple: *balancé*, a *pirouette*, and a *grand plié*.

While the others struggled, Gracie mastered it in minutes.

"Nice, Gracie." Miss Noreen wrote on her clipboard. "You pick choreography up quickly."

"It's easy-peasy." Gracie smiled. Mr. Minnelli couldn't help but chuckle.

"Do you want to try something that's not so easy-peasy?" he asked her.

"Sure!" Gracie beamed. "Bring it on!"

He nodded at Miss Noreen, who asked the rest of the group to take a seat while she taught Gracie a combination.

"Now take it slow," she instructed her. "It's very complicated." She did the step alongside her as she called out, "*En face ballonné devant*, step left, *coupé derrière sauté*, step right, *coupé derrière sauté!*"

The other kids scratched their heads, but Gracie mimicked her perfectly. At the end, she gave a graceful curtsy. "How was that?" she asked Mr. Minnelli.

"Fine. Fine indeed!" he said, impressed. "Where do you study?"

"In my bedroom mostly—sometimes on the couch but my mom says I shouldn't do my homework while watching TV 'cause then I don't pay attention and I get the answers wrong."

Miss Andrea and Miss Noreen both giggled. Mr. Minnelli cleared his throat. "No, dear, I mean where do you study dance?"

"Oh! Why didn't you say so?" Gracie replied. "At Dance Divas. My teacher is Miss Toni and she's fantabulously talented and really pretty and she let me join the team with my sister, Scoot."

Mr. Minnelli raised an eyebrow. "You have a sister named Scoot?"

"Well, I call her Scoot, but it's really Scarlett. Scoot's *funner*, don't you think?"

"I do." Mr. Minnelli nodded. "And I think you may just be the *funnest* audition I have seen so far today."

Gracie smiled wide. "Can I have some candy now?"

✳ ✳ ✳

Meanwhile, in studio one, Liberty and Anya were waiting for their turn to dance.

"Look at her posture." Liberty pointed out a girl who scrunched her shoulders up as she did sixteen *changements* in a row. "Hideous!"

A tall man with wavy dark hair and steel-blue eyes came in and sat on a stool in front of the room.

"Do you think that's . . . ," Anya asked.

"Miss Toni's old boyfriend?" Liberty finished her sentence. "Only one way to find out!"

Liberty raised her hand. "Excuse me," she said sweetly. "We're from the Dance Divas Studio in Scotch Plains, New Jersey, and Miss Antoinette Moore told us to tell you hi."

The man looked up from his notebook. "You study with Toni?" he asked, surprised.

Liberty smirked and elbowed Anya. "Mission accomplished. That is *definitely* Marcus Sanzobar."

⟦ 22 ⟧

Marcus rose from his stool. "Well, I would expect Toni's dancers to be the very best . . . ," he began.

Liberty smiled. "Of course we are. At least I am."

Marcus's face got suddenly stern. "And I'd also expect them to be a little more respectful and modest."

He turned to face the rest of the dancers. "And now if there are no more interruptions, I'd like to get on with the auditions."

Anya gulped. "Nice job, Liberty. He hates us already."

In studio two, things weren't going much better for Scarlett, Rochelle, and Hayden. Miss Andrea walked in and immediately began putting them through their paces.

"Relax those hands. Keep that head tall," Miss Andrea reminded Rochelle. "You!" she pointed at Scarlett. "You were wobbly on that *piqué en dedans*! Strong legs!"

Hayden's *tour chaînés* looked great—until another dancer accidentally spun into him and knocked him over. "Watch where you're going!" the boy yelled at him.

"Me? I'm not the klutz! Why don't you look where you're going—and stay off my feet!" Hayden replied.

Miss Andrea sighed. "I have to say I was hoping for more from the elite Dance Divas competitive team," she said.

Scarlett shot Rochelle a worried look. Miss Toni expected all of them to get leads in *The Nutcracker.* Scarlett wondered if any of them would even make it into the cast!

* * *

Bria was doing her best in studio three to follow the intricate *tendu* and *pirouette* combination that Miss Becky, another one of the Dances Minnelli ballet mistresses, had demonstrated for them. But she couldn't remember if the count started on six or on five, and if she should start with her right or left. She chose wrong.

"Why are you going left when everyone else is going right?" Miss Becky asked her. "You're a beat behind."

"I'm sorry. Could you just go over it one more time?"

Bria wished that at least one of her Diva teammates could be in the studio with her. She could always look over to Scarlett or Rock and they'd help her get back in sync with the routine. Here, she felt like the odd dancer out. None of the other girls were going to offer her any hints or help—not when there were principal roles at stake.

"One more time from the top," Miss Becky said. "And anyone who doesn't get it this time, please take a seat. We can't waste time on people who can't keep up."

Bria's eyes grew wide.

She knew Miss Becky meant her.

CHAPTER 4

Tiny Dancer

Miss Andrea had explained that it would be at least a week before Dances Minnelli made any decisions on the casting.

"Did you check your e-mail again?" Anya asked Bria. They were all gathered around her laptop in the dressing room at Dance Divas. "It's Saturday. It's been exactly a week. We should have the cast list by now!"

Bria hit Refresh on her mailbox for the third time. "Nope. Nothing."

"This is so stressful!" Anya groaned. "What's taking so long?"

"They're probably trying to decide if I'd make a better Clara or Sugar Plum," Liberty said, pulling on a pair of leg warmers. "It's a tough call."

Bria hit the button one more time. "Still nothing."

"My mom always says 'a watched pot never boils,'" Scarlett pointed out.

"She says that when she's cooking spaghetti," Gracie chimed in.

"What's that supposed to mean?" Rochelle asked.

Scarlett grabbed her friend's arm and pulled her off the bench. "It means stop waiting for the e-mail and get to dance class. We can check it later."

Just then, a chime sounded on Bria's computer.

"You've got mail! You've got mail!" Anya said excitedly. "What is it?"

Bria checked her inbox. There was an e-mail from Miss Andrea with the subject: "Congratulations!"

"What are you waiting for? Click on it!" Liberty screamed.

"Oh, I thought you weren't worried," Rochelle taunted her. "Maybe we should just hold off until after technique class . . ."

Liberty grabbed the laptop away from Bria and opened the e-mail. Her jaw dropped.

"What? What is it?" Anya begged. "Read it! The suspense is killing me!"

Liberty was utterly speechless. She turned the laptop toward Scarlett. "You read it."

Scarlett looked at the screen. It was a long letter from Miss Andrea congratulating everyone who had been cast in this year's *A New Jersey Nutcracker*. Then there was the official cast list with a familiar name right at the top of it.

"Gracie?" Scarlett gasped.

"Yeah?" Gracie asked. "What is it, Scoot?"

"You're Clara. You—you actually got the role of Clara."

Gracie screamed and ran around the dressing room, doing cartwheels. "I did it! I'm Clara! I'm Clara!"

Scarlett read the rest of the list. "Bria and I

are snowflakes; Anya is a mouse; Rochelle and Hayden are soldiers. And Liberty . . ."

"Is a gingerbread man? Ridiculous!" Liberty said. "Mr. Minnelli needs a new pair of glasses. I'm going to have my mother call and demand he make some changes this instant! How can I be a gingerbread man while Gracie gets to be Clara?"

Though she wasn't thrilled with her part, Scarlett did have to defend her little sister. "Gracie earned it, fair and square," she told Liberty. "She had what they were looking for, and you have to accept it."

"I'm gonna go find Miss Toni and tell her!" Gracie said, racing out of the dressing room. "I'm Clara! I'm Clara!"

"You are never going to hear the end of this," Rochelle said. "If there's anything Gracie does super well, it's gloating."

"I can just hear my mom now: 'be happy for your little sister,'" Scarlett replied. "I am happy for her. I'm just sad for me. I always dreamed of playing Clara. Gracie didn't even know what *The Nutcracker* was until last week!"

"Look on the bright side," Bria said. "We all got cast. That will make Miss Toni happy. Even if they're not all leads."

When they came into the studio for class, Toni was already congratulating Gracie. "I'm so proud of you," she said, hugging her. "As for the rest of you . . ."

She turned to face the group. "Did you see who got the role of the Sugar Plum Fairy?"

"It wasn't listed yet. It said it was still to be determined," Anya replied.

"Well, it was just determined. I got an e-mail from Justine Chase, rubbing it in my face. Her student Addison is playing Sugar Plum."

"Addison wasn't even at the auditions," Liberty insisted. "Something stinks like Smelly Feet!"

"And she's not even from New Jersey—she's from New York!" Gracie protested. "She shouldn't get to play a fairy in the *NEW JERSEY Nutcracker*."

"Maybe Justine called her old *pas de deux*

partner Marcus and asked him for a favor," Rochelle suggested. "It would be so like her to try and outdo the Divas."

"What's done is done," Toni said and sniffed. "At least Gracie did what she was supposed to do."

"We did try," Anya insisted. "We did our best."

"Who cares about the stupid *Nutcracker*? I'm not doing some lame role," Liberty said.

"Oh, yes, you are." Miss Toni stood up and placed her hands on her hips. "Every one of you is doing that show, and you are going to make the best of it. Divas don't quit. I won't allow it."

"That's not fair," Liberty sulked. "I hate my part."

"You get what you get and don't get upset," Rochelle teased her. "I bet you'll make a cute gingerbread dude." She waddled around with stiff arms and legs.

"That's enough," Toni said, cutting her off. "There are no small parts, just small dancers."

"I'm a small dancer." Gracie giggled. "But I'm Clara!"

Toni smiled. "You are indeed. Looks like Gracie won this round, hands down. Only one question remains: who will be your prince?"

"That's right! They didn't list the name of the Nutcracker Prince!" Scarlett exclaimed.

Gracie gulped. "You don't suppose they'll make me dance the whole time by myself, do you?" she asked Miss Toni. Gracie was always full of confidence in any group number, duo, or trio. But when she had to take the spotlight by herself, stage fright set in.

"Rest assured, there will be a Nutcracker in *The Nutcracker*," Miss Toni told her. "I just wonder what—or who—Marcus has up his sleeve."

* *
*

Rehearsals started immediately the next day at Dances Minnelli Studio—there was no time to waste. They all had to learn the choreography, get fitted for their costumes, and have everything ready for the holiday audiences in seven short weeks.

"I know it's a lot for you to learn," Mr. Minnelli told Gracie. "But I'm confident you can do it."

"Of course I can!" Gracie answered. "One time, Miss Toni had me learn a duet in two hours for a major competition in Atlanta and I did it, no sweat. Don't worry, Mr. Minnelli. I've got your back."

The choreographer smiled. "I have no doubt about that, young lady. Just bring that energy and confidence to your role and we'll be in great shape."

"And you," he turned to Addison. "I'm counting on you to be a breathtaking Sugar Plum. You come highly recommended."

"I told you!" Rochelle elbowed Scarlett. "I knew Justine was behind this."

"We don't know that for sure," Bria reminded her. "Addison *is* a really good dancer."

"I'm just as good," Liberty said. "Better. I don't scrunch up my face when I'm concentrating."

They watched as Addison glided across the floor in her toe shoes, as light as if she were dancing on clouds. "I hate to admit it, but she's good," Rochelle remarked. "*Really* good."

Liberty put her hands over her ears. "I am not listening to this! It's bad enough we have to be in this silly show. Now I have to play second fiddle to one of the Stinky Feet?"

Bria nodded. "I'm used to it. My sister is amazing at everything she does. I'm always a step behind her."

Scarlett glanced over at Gracie, who was twirling around the stage, holding a red-and-gold painted nutcracker in her hands as the rest of the children in the party scene reached for it. It felt strange for her to play "second fiddle" to her little sister. In the past, it had always been Scarlett who was in the lead. Now Gracie was getting all the attention.

"Like this?" she asked Marcus as she pretended to cradle the nutcracker in her arms like a baby.

"Exactly!" he replied. "You're worried about the Nutcracker being broken. You're sad that he's hurt."

Gracie's eyes welled with tears. "It's okay, little Nutcracker," she whispered. "I'm here." Her face looked both tender and brave.

Mr. Minnelli dabbed his eyes with a handkerchief. "Lovely, just lovely," he said. "You're a natural actress. The rest of you, please stand on the sidelines while we go over Clara and the prince's duet. You," he said, pointing to Hayden, "you stand in for the prince."

Scarlett shuffled off to a corner. This was not going to be easy. Rochelle read her mind. "How do you think I feel?" she whispered. "I wanted those roles so badly for me and Hayden."

"Why do you think the Nutcracker Prince is MIA?" Bria asked them. "Mr. Minnelli hasn't said a word about who he might be."

"I bet it's some big-time ballet star," Anya said, speculating. "Like Chase Finlay or Jared Angle."

Rochelle shrugged. "I don't know who either of those dudes are, but who do you think that little pip-squeak is?" She pointed to the studio entrance, where a tiny boy in a fedora hat was standing with his mother. His nose was pressed up against the glass door.

Mr. Minnelli noticed him at the same time. "Ah, yes! Here at last! Please come in!" He motioned for the boy to enter the studio.

"Everyone," Mr. Minnelli announced, "I would like you to meet Olivier Mason from Central Delaware Youth Ballet. He is going to be our Nutcracker Prince!"

Rochelle's jaw dropped to the floor. "Seriously? This little munchkin is the prince? Is he even out of diapers yet?" She gazed over at Hayden, who looked just as shocked. Mr. Minnelli had practically shoved him to the side to make room for Olivier.

Bria elbowed her. "Check it out."

Olivier was extending his hand for Gracie to shake it. "It's a pleasure to meet you," he said.

Gracie scratched her head. "Um, hi, Oliver," she replied.

The boy pulled his hand away. "No, not

Oliver. *Oh-liv-ee-ay*. Like the famous actor Laurence Olivier."

Gracie's face lit up. "Oh, I get it! O-live-ee-YAY! Cool name!"

The boy seemed pleased and took his spot next to Gracie.

Scarlett chuckled. No wonder they chose her little sis to play Clara. They needed someone who was actually shorter than the prince!

Olivier took off his hat and began stretching out on the floor. "His feet are pretty sick," Rochelle commented. "Look at that arch! And he's so flexible." They watched as the little boy did an effortless split, then pressed his forehead to his knee.

Anya nodded. "He's like a human pretzel. Impressive, I gotta admit."

Liberty had been silent the entire time. "This ballet is a joke," she barked. "Clara and the prince look like they belong in kindergarten, and I'm playing a walking pastry!"

"A cookie, technically," Bria corrected her. "Gingerbread men are cookies."

Liberty practically snarled at her. "If it weren't for Toni's stupid rule that we had to do this show, I'd be out the door."

As much as she hated to agree with her, Anya felt the same way. "Better a cookie than a rodent."

CHAPTER 5

That's the Way the Cookie Crumbles

The gingerbread scene was the most comical in the ballet. As lead gingerbread, Liberty had to duck under Mother Ginger's huge hoop skirt and leap out at the audience.

"Let me get this straight," Liberty said, complaining to Marcus. "You want me to crawl on the floor under some granny's skirt and then pop out and make a complete fool out of myself?"

Marcus rested his hands on his hips. "If you choose to make a complete fool out of yourself, then that's your decision. I expect you to burst onto the stage exuding joy and excitement. If you can't handle that, there's the door."

"Ooh, I like him," Rochelle whispered to Scarlett. "Anyone who disses Liberty gets my vote!"

"Fine," Liberty said, taking her place. "I am a professional."

"The lead gingerbread has to really ham it up," Miss Noreen instructed her.

"That won't be a problem for Liberty." Rochelle chuckled.

Miss Noreen showed her the choreography, a combination of *arabesques*, *pirouettes*, and something that resembled a waddling penguin.

"Elbows should be shoulder level, palms open wide," she demonstrated.

The other gingerbread dancers looked cute and funny as they raced around the studio. Liberty looked mean and ornery and practically bit Mother Ginger's head off when she got too close.

"Gingerbread don't growl," Marcus corrected Liberty. "You're supposed to be smiling."

"I'm supposed to be Clara," Liberty muttered under her breath. "This is totally humiliating."

At the end of the scene, Liberty had to turn

her back to the audience so Mother Ginger could give her a playful kick.

"No way," Liberty said, crossing her arms over her chest. "I am not getting my butt kicked in a ballet."

"Oh, this is a dream come true!" Rochelle roared with laughter.

Scarlett was enjoying every minute of the dance as well—especially when Liberty had to do a somersault and land facedown on the stage with her arms and legs wide apart.

"Gingerbread go SPLAT!" Anya said, cracking up.

"This is a riot!" Bria added. "I'm gonna post it on Instagram!"

Liberty spotted her teammates laughing at her and stopped in her tracks.

"It's not funny!" she screamed at them.

"No, it *is* funny," Marcus insisted. "It's brilliant. Liberty, you have great comic timing. I could see you playing Coppélia one day."

Liberty's scowl softened. "Wait. Really?"

"Absolutely," he answered. "It'll be even funnier when we get you in the big brown suit."

Liberty rolled her eyes. Even if Marcus thought she had prima ballerina potential, this was the most embarrassing role she had ever danced.

"About the costume," she said to Marcus. "Would you mind if I made a few tweaks? My mom just met Katy Perry at a party in Hollywood, and I know Katy would be totally cool with lending me some of her wardrobe . . ."

"Yes," Marcus huffed.

"Yes, I can call Katy?"

"Yes, I would mind if you tweaked your costume. I am the director and I am the only person who tweaks anything around here. Now, get your butt back on the floor—literally."

Gracie wasn't paying much attention to Liberty's tantrums. She and Olivier were getting along fabulously—thanks to an icebreaker that Miss Noreen insisted they play to get to know each other.

While the others rehearsed, they sat in a corner, asking each other crazy questions.

"What's the grossest pizza you ever tasted?" Olivier challenged Gracie.

"Oh, that's an easy one: barbecue chicken with marshmallows."

"Eww!" Olivier cracked up. "Now you go."

"Funnest day ever?" Gracie asked.

Olivier tapped his finger to his nose. "Give me a sec. I'm thinking . . ."

"Ten seconds," Gracie warned him. "Miss Noreen said ten seconds to answer."

"Catching a foul ball at the Wilmington Blue Rocks game and eating six hot dogs at Frawley Stadium. I could have gone for seven, but my mom worried I'd throw up."

Gracie's eyes widened. "You like hot dogs?"

Olivier nodded. "With ketchup, relish, onions, mustard . . . the works."

It was as if he had said the magic words. In Gracie's mind, no food on the planet could top hot dogs. Her dad always made them for her on his backyard grill. She could eat them for breakfast, lunch, and dinner and never get bored.

"I love hot dogs," she gushed. "My record is nine—but the last one had no bun, so I don't think that really counts."

"Nuh-uh." Olivier shook his head. "For the official count, it has to be bunned. Maybe we can have a dog eat-off sometime?"

Gracie smiled and they pinky swore on it. Clearly, Mr. Minnelli had been right in casting them together. It was a match made in hot dog heaven.

CHAPTER 6

New Boy on the Block

That night at dinner, Scarlett could hardly get a word in as Gracie told her mom all about the first rehearsal.

"I get to do a dance with the dolls, Mommy," she said. "And the Nutcracker eats hot dogs with ketchup!" She dipped a fish stick in a puddle of ketchup to illustrate.

Their mom looked confused. "Aren't nutcrackers supposed to eat nuts, honey? Isn't that the point?"

"She means Olivier, the boy who's playing the Nutcracker," Scarlett explained. "They're two of a kind. He's seven, short, and he's a hot dog freak like Gracie."

"We are not freaks," Gracie protested. "Plus, he said he'll be eight in two weeks and he's not short—he's taller than me."

"By an inch maybe!" Scarlett chuckled. "It was absolutely hilarious, Mom! Marcus, the director, was shouting for them, and they were right there under his nose. He just had to look down to see them!"

Her mom tried not to laugh. "It sounds adorable, Gracie. Really."

"You're just making fun of us because you're jealous," Gracie fired back at her sister. "You wanted to be Clara, and I got the part because I'm better than you are!"

Scarlett was about to toss back an insult, when she considered what Gracie had said. Was it possible that she was right? That she was, in fact, a better dancer? In all these years, she'd always been the better one, but now Gracie was getting good—very good. Didn't landing this lead role in *The Nutcracker* prove it?

"See! You're not saying anything because you know it's true," Gracie said, pushing her plate away from her. "Can I be done, Mom? I have to go practice my tree-growing scene."

"Homework first," her mom warned her. "And I don't want you girls fighting over this. I'm very proud of you both."

Scarlett shrugged. She didn't feel very proud of herself. So far, her routine consisted of pretending to "fall" around the stage and look graceful doing it. She was one of fifteen snowflakes—just a face in the crowd.

"This is her moment, Scarlett," her mom said, clearing the plates. "You have to let her shine. It's only fair. You've had a lot of moments over the years. Now it's Gracie's turn."

Scarlett knew that was true, but it still didn't make her feel any better.

* * *

When Scarlett got to Dance Divas Studio the next day, Anya was waiting for her in the dressing room and looked equally frustrated.

"Whiskers," she told her friend. "I seriously have to wear whiskers! And there's like a gazillion other mice racing around onstage. In those ears and that furry gray suit, you can't tell one of us from the other."

Scarlett peeled off her layers of coat, scarf, and sweater, and nodded. "I know. I feel the same way. But both my mom and Miss Toni keep saying to just make the most of it and do my best."

Anya shook her head. "How am I supposed to do my best when I feel like I should have been given another part? I've had Sugar Plum dreams my whole life. Addison squashed them."

"But there's nothing that says that dream is over." Scarlett tried to sound optimistic. "There's always next year."

"I can't even think about tomorrow, much less next year." Anya sighed. "We rehearsed the battle scene yesterday, and I'm the first mouse to die. I have to lie on my back with my legs twitching while the others carry me off the stage. They might as well list me in the program as 'Dead Mouse Number One'!"

Scarlett giggled. "Okay, that is just a little funny, don't you think?"

"I see nothing amusing in mouse murder," Anya replied. "And what's worse is that Rochelle is the one that kills me with her sword."

As if on cue, Rochelle burst into the dressing room. "Straight through the heart!" she said, brandishing her umbrella like a sword. "Take that Mickey—you're going down!"

"I prefer Minnie, thank you," Anya said. "And could you not enjoy it so much?"

"What am I supposed to do? Mope around because I didn't get a big part like Gracie or Addison?"

Anya nodded. "Moping works for me."

"I can't be sad, especially when there's a huge chance of a snow day tomorrow. No school! No rehearsals!" Rochelle exclaimed.

"A snow day in early November?" Bria said, overhearing the conversation as she walked in.

"When's the last time that happened?" She searched on her computer and came up with one ten years ago in her school district. "It has to be a foot of snow for them to even consider it. And all they're predicting is some flurries."

"Maybe you and Scarlett can do your snowflake dance for us and bring it on," Rochelle teased.

"I've never heard of a snowflake dance," Bria replied. "I think you mean a Native American rain dance."

"What I think is that you all take things way too seriously," Rochelle replied. "Look on the bright side: Gracie will probably freeze onstage like she always does, and they'll know better than to put a little kid in a big part next year."

Scarlett, Bria, and Anya laughed alongside Rochelle.

But suddenly Rochelle noticed Gracie standing behind her. Gracie's cheeks were bright red, and she looked like she was about to cry.

"Gracie! I'm so sorry!" Rochelle apologized. "I didn't know you were standing there."

"I am not going to freeze onstage," Gracie said slowly, choking back tears. "I am going to be an amazing Clara. I'll show you!" Then she looked at Scarlett. "I thought you were happy for me."

"Gracie! Wait!" Scarlett tried to run after her but it was no use. Gracie felt like they had all betrayed her.

"She's right," Scarlett told the girls. "We aren't acting like teammates or friends. We're only feeling sorry for ourselves. We should be cheering Gracie on."

When they got to class, Liberty and Gracie were already lined up and stretching in front of the mirrors. Scarlett tapped her sister on the shoulder. "Gracie, we're really sorry," she whispered. "Please don't be upset!"

Gracie ignored her and stared straight ahead.

"Gracie told me what you all said," Liberty defended her. "I think it's just dreadful and we don't wish to speak with you at this time."

Rochelle couldn't believe what she was hearing. "Hold on a Sugar Plum second! Are you actually being *nice* to Gracie? Since when are you nice to anyone?"

Liberty put her arm around Gracie. "Of course I'm being nice. What are friends for?" She smiled sweetly. "Right, bestie?" She escorted Gracie to a corner where they could stretch in private.

"Okay, that's weird," Bria said, watching Liberty flex and point Gracie's toes for her on the floor.

"Very weird," Rochelle added. "I smell a rat."

Anya groaned. "I'm a mouse, not a rat."

"I'm not talking about you," Rochelle explained. "I mean Liberty. Why is she cozying up to Gracie all of a sudden?"

"Maybe she really does feel bad that we were mean about her getting Clara?" Scarlett suggested. "I mean, I feel bad."

Rochelle shook her head. "No way. Liberty's got something up her sleeve, I can feel it."

Just then, Miss Toni came into the room. She was shadowed by a small boy in a bright blue fedora. "You all know Olivier," she said without glancing up from her clipboard. "He's going to be taking some classes with us while he's doing *A New Jersey Nutcracker*." She pointed to a spot on the floor and Olivier raced to fill it.

"I thought you live in Delaware," Bria asked him. "Isn't it far for you to come to our studio every day?"

"I do live in Delaware, but I'm staying with my uncle Marcus while I do the show." He began doing deep *pliés*.

Rochelle's mouth dropped. "What? Your uncle is Marcus Sanzobar? No wonder you got the lead."

"Rock!" Scarlett hushed her. "That isn't nice."

"No, it's not," Rochelle replied. "It isn't nice to cast someone just because they're family! That's called nepotism. Google it on Bria's computer if you don't believe me."

She was shouting and now had everyone's attention—even Miss Toni's.

"It's called talent," her teacher said firmly. "Have you seen Olivier dance? He's far better than his uncle was as a teenager—and he's only seven years old."

Olivier raised his hand. "I'll be eight soon."

Toni walked over to Rochelle. "That is the last nasty comment I want to hear in this studio. Is that clear?"

Rochelle stared down at her feet. "Yeah."

"We may not be competing as a dance team at the moment, but the cast of any show is a team as well," Toni added. "You support each other and you applaud each other."

Scarlett looked over at Gracie, who was still ignoring her. Miss Toni's scolding made her feel even worse for putting her little sister down.

Liberty raised her hand. "Miss Toni, I think we should have a birthday and 'Welcome to the Divas' party for Olivier. I'd be happy to throw it at my house."

"Yay! A party!" Gracie jumped up and down. "Can I come?"

"You can all come," Liberty said, smiling. "The more, the merrier! We have a huge house, so we can invite the whole *Nutcracker* cast and crew."

Rochelle was about to say something when

Scarlett gave her a light kick. "Remember what Toni said," she whispered. "No more nasty comments."

"I think that would be a lovely gesture," Toni told Liberty. "Olivier, is it all right with you?"

The boy mulled it over. "Can we have hot dogs? And an ice cream cake with those chocolate crunchies in the middle?"

Liberty nodded. "Gracie and I will do all the planning and make sure it's absolutely perfect."

Gracie hugged Liberty, and Scarlett sighed. The only thing she could do now was hope the party didn't turn out to be a perfect disaster.

CHAPTER 7

Spaced Out

Gracie insisted that the theme of Olivier's eighth birthday party be something that he loved.

"He's really into space and astronauts," she informed Liberty. "He's been to the planetarium in New York City a gazillion times. And he loves freeze-dried astronaut ice cream."

Liberty rubbed her temples. "I am not serving freeze-dried food at my par—I mean *Olivier's* party," she said. "We'll have to come up with a better menu. But I'm okay with the outer space thing. It's kinda retro."

"Can we make some invitations and put little gold star stickers on them?" Gracie suggested.

Again, Liberty shot her idea down. "Stickers? What are we, first graders?"

Gracie shook her head. "No, I'm in second grade!"

"What I mean is that we need to do something for Olivier that is more special. I'll call my mom's party planner and get back to you."

*
* *

The next day at Dance Divas Studio, Gracie was still not talking to any of her teammates except Liberty.

"I like your new leotard," Anya said, complimenting Gracie. "What do you call that color? Robin's egg blue?"

Gracie ignored her and continued putting on her jazz shoes.

"My mom made me a strawberry-mango-banana smoothie," Bria said. "Want some, Gracie?"

Again, nothing.

It was as if they were talking to a brick wall.

Liberty skipped into the dressing room, red envelopes in hand. "Here ya go," she said, distributing them. "RSVPs required." She took Gracie's hand as they strolled out of the dressing room together.

Anya opened the envelope. Inside was a formal invitation printed in gold type:

3-2-1-BLASTOFF for
OLIVIER'S 8th BIRTHDAY!

WHEN: Saturday, November 15, 3:00 p.m.

WHERE: Chez Liberty,
1 Rattlesnake Road, Alpine, New Jersey

ATTIRE: Space Chic!

Luncheon will be served

Rochelle read the invitation a second time. "Does anyone else find it fitting that Liberty lives on Rattlesnake Road? She's such a snake!"

"What's 'space chic'?" Bria asked. "Do I have to dress like Chewbacca?"

Scarlett didn't know what to say or think.

On the one hand, it was very generous of Liberty to throw such an extravagant party for Olivier. On the other hand, she probably had other motives.

"I think we should go as the Divanauts," she said.

"You mean matching astronaut costumes?" Bria asked.

"We are a team aren't we?" Anya asked. "I like that idea a lot, and I volunteer to help make them."

"Maybe we can even put together a dance to perform for Olivier at the party," Rochelle suggested.

Scarlett checked the calendar on her phone. "We have no *Nutcracker* rehearsal tomorrow night. So everybody come over to my place and we'll get sewing and dancing."

* * *

Scarlett put a bag of popcorn into the microwave. "The girls are gonna be here any minute, Mom!" she called into the living room. "Are we ready?"

Her mother was busy fishing her sewing machine out of the closet. "I think so."

Gracie was watching her favorite TV show, *Extreme Fast Food*, on the Travel Channel when Scarlett came in carrying a large bowl of hot buttered popcorn.

"Help yourself, Gracie." She tried to make peace with her sister. "Do you want to be a Divanaut with us?"

Gracie shook her head. "Liberty and I are going as Martian twins," she said. "Lady Gaga's costume designer is making us red, glittery alien outfits."

Scarlett tried to sound enthusiastic. "Cool! You and Liberty are, uh, twins." She looked at her mom and mouthed, "HELP!"

"Honey, I know you like Liberty," her mom began, "but don't you think it would be nice to do something with *all* the girls on the team, not just her?"

Gracie got up and started walking toward her bedroom. "I wanna be a Martian," she said, calling back. "Divanauts are dumb."

Just then the doorbell rang. "Got it!" Scarlett said, racing to let her friends in. "Who's feeling spacey?" she asked as she opened the door.

"ME!" Anya, Rochelle, and Bria all shouted in unison. The girls set up camp on the couch.

"I found these cool USA flag patches at the craft store," Bria said, opening her purse. "How awesome would these look on our space suits?"

"Love it!" Scarlett replied. "Bria, did you do the research?"

Bria pulled out a folder filled with photos of authentic astronaut uniforms and gear. "I think we should have white jumpsuits with silver pockets and a big zipper down the front," she said.

"Let's make the jumpsuits short—like shorts we'd wear for a dance class," Rochelle suggested. She had a pile of their old group costumes she found in the studio storage closet—white shorts and crop tops they'd worn for a "Going to the Chapel" wedding routine. "If we stitch them together and put on some trim and embellishments, I think it'll work."

They all agreed and started sewing using Scarlett's mom's machine. After a few hours, they were done and tried them on for size.

Anya admired herself in the bathroom mirror. "These are great. I hope Miss Toni doesn't notice we did a little fashion makeover on our old costumes."

Scarlett agreed. "We look the part. Now we need a fabulous dance routine to perform."

Bria held up her phone. "I downloaded the perfect music."

At the touch of a button, an eerie voice filled the room: "Space, the final frontier . . ." Then Frank Sinatra's version of "Fly Me to the Moon" started playing.

Rochelle covered her ears. "Oh, no, no, no! Not cool at all!" she said. "My grandma likes that song."

Bria pouted. "I thought my *Star Trek*/Sinatra remix was very cool," she insisted. "I don't suppose you have any better ideas?"

"How about Katy Perry's 'E.T.'?" Rochelle

suggested. "No one's cooler than Katy, and it has a spacey vibe."

Both Anya and Scarlett agreed.

"Fine." Bria sniffed. "I'm outvoted. But I think you could have at least given Frank a chance!"

CHAPTER 8

Birthday Blastoff

Scarlett knew that any party Liberty threw would be over-the-top—but this one was over-the-moon. When she and the rest of the Divas arrived, they were greeted by several servers dressed in various alien costumes. Liberty's mom, Jane, was dressed in a gold hooded jumpsuit with matching metallic eye shadow and lipstick.

"Hi, girls!" She waved. "Just call me J-3PO!"

Rochelle rolled her eyes. "Oh boy. This is gonna be interesting."

"I like the dude with green skin and three eyes," Bria remarked. "He kinda looks like my uncle Charles . . ."

A woman with pink hair and antennas offered Anya an appetizer. "Pig in a rocket?" she asked, waving the plate under her nose. Anya took a mini hot dog wrapped in a roll with a triangular hunk of cheese on top. "This is so Gracie," she told Scarlett. "It's just too much!"

"Don't you mean *tutu* much?" Rochelle teased. "A little ballet humor."

Scarlett looked around for Gracie. She insisted her mom drive her over early to help Liberty with all the last-minute details and Scarlett hadn't seen her since. She wasn't by the platter of star fruit and Mars red velvet cookies, nor was she playing the Saturn's ring toss game in the living room. At least the birthday boy was having a blast: Olivier was zapping "alien invaders" on the giant TV in Liberty's den.

"You know what's missing from this party?" Rochelle asked her friends.

"Darth Vader?" Bria replied, stuffing a flying saucer–shaped ice cream sandwich in her mouth.

"No, our humble hostess," Rock replied. "I haven't seen Liberty anywhere."

"Or Gracie," Scarlett pointed out.

Just then, one of the four-armed, blue-skinned aliens summoned everyone. "Aliens and astronauts, may I call your attention to the formal dining room," he said. Everyone filed in to see what was happening.

There, in the middle of the room, was a giant "moon rock"—craters and all.

"Awesome!" Olivier said, knocking on it. "This is so cool!"

"Stand back," the alien announcer advised him. The room went dark as a laser light show began spinning on the ceiling. Then, in a flash of smoke, the moon rock cracked in half. Out came Gracie and Liberty—the Martian twins—in matching red sequin bodysuits and flowing red wigs. Katy Perry's "E.T." boomed over the speakers.

"That's our song! They stole our song!" Rochelle exclaimed.

Liberty and Gracie did an amazing acrobatic duet filled with flips, spins, and tricks. The crowd applauded wildly.

"We can't do our dance now—we'll look like copycats," Bria whispered to her teammates.

"All that work for nothing. You think it was a coincidence?" Rochelle asked Scarlett. "Or did Gracie eavesdrop and rat us out?"

Scarlett had to admit it was pretty fishy—and just like Liberty to put her little sis up to something so sneaky and underhanded.

"It doesn't matter," she said and sighed. "Olivier is happy and that's what counts. It's not about our dance; it's about his party."

Rochelle glanced over at Liberty, who was bowing and blowing kisses to the party guests. "Really? I think it's all about Liberty—as usual."

CHAPTER 9

Get to the Pointe

With only two more weeks to practice before opening night, Mr. Minnelli was feeling the pressure to get everything in his ballet perfect. He mopped his brow with a white handkerchief and exclaimed things like, *"Quelle horreur!"* whenever the dancers forgot a step, bent their knees, or fell a beat behind the music.

All rehearsals now took place at the Paramus Playhouse on the massive stage. There was so much to remember, and so many little details to check: the lights, the sets, the Ferris wheel, not to mention that all of the dances had to go off without a hitch.

The "Russian Dance" from the Land of Sweets was one of the hardest to execute. It involved crazy acrobat leaps, flips, and stunts.

Marcus clapped his hands together. "Where are my Russians?" Three boys—Will, Ben, and Presley—appeared onstage.

"This is one of the most memorable dances of the entire production," he said to them. "Let's hope it's for a good reason . . ."

The music pounded from the loudspeakers and the dancers rushed out onto the stage, leaping and flipping through the air.

"More energy!" Marcus shouted. "Those split jumps should be high enough to touch the sky!"

But the more Marcus barked, the more confused they got. Ben accidentally tumbled into Presley, who tripped Will just as he was about to do his cartwheel. They all landed in a heap on the stage.

"Tragic, tragic, tragic," Mr. Minnelli moaned. "Can't anyone here do a decent flip without falling flat on his face?"

"Gracie can!" Liberty said, peeking out from

the wings. She gave her a little push. "She could do that dance in her sleep. She's an amazing gymnast."

Gracie gulped. All eyes were staring at her. "I am?"

"Totally!" Liberty gave her another shove. "She can show you how it should be done."

"You don't say?" Mr. Minnelli replied, raising an eyebrow. "Would you care to show us, Gracie?"

Gracie walked to stage right and waited for the music to start. She executed a perfect aerial cartwheel and then squatted on the floor with her arms crossed over her chest. She kicked her legs out to either side without a single wobble.

"*Spasibo!*" Mr. Minnelli cheered. "That's Russian for 'thank you.' That, gentlemen, is what I want to see!"

Gracie beamed as the cast applauded.

"Great job," Liberty whispered. "You are the best dancer here."

"Really?" Gracie said. "You think I'm better than even you?"

Liberty gritted her teeth. "Well, I wouldn't go

that far . . ." Then she smiled sweetly. "But you're the star, Gracie. And as the star, you should get everything you want."

"What do you mean?" Gracie asked.

Liberty noticed the crew working on the Land of Sweets backdrop. They were hard at work creating a mosaic out of multicolored candies that spelled out "Welcome to the Shore."

"You see those candies over there?" She pointed to a mountain of gummy bears, lollipops, and jellybeans scattered on a table backstage.

"Yeah! Yum!" Gracie said, licking her lips. "There must be a gazillion of them."

"Right, so you certainly help yourself to as many as you want," Liberty said, egging her on.

Gracie's eyes grew wide. "I can? I mean, I can!" She marched over and scooped up a pile and began popping them in her mouth. There were so many different kinds for the taking.

"Hey, what are you doing?" one of the scenic designers asked her. "Drop those props right now! Those are property of *A New Jersey Nutcracker*!"

"And I'm the star of *A New Jersey Nutcracker*," Gracie insisted, swiping another handful off the table. "So I can have them."

Scarlett overheard the exchange and raced over. "Gracie! Give 'em back!" she pleaded.

"Nuh-uh," her little sister replied, taking a bite out of a red licorice twist. "Liberty says I can have as much as I want."

"I'm so sorry," Scarlett said, apologizing. "She didn't understand this was for decoration, not eating. She won't take any more."

"I *did* understand." Gracie stamped her foot. "I'm the star and I make the rules." She marched away in a huff, leaving a trail of jellybeans behind her.

"What was that all about?" Rochelle asked.

Scarlett shook her head. "I don't know. But whatever it is, Liberty's behind it."

CHAPTER 10

Scene and Heard

"I want to run the snow scene," Mr. Minnelli called from the back row of the theater. "How are we doing with the flakes?"

"Does he mean us?" Bria asked Scarlett.

Scarlett pointed to a box of white confetti floating high above their heads. "I think that's what he means. It's a snow machine."

On cue, delicate white flakes wafted down from the ceiling. "Cue the music!" Mr. Minnelli shouted.

The "Waltz of the Snowflakes" song filled the air.

"Too loud!" Marcus yelled to the sound crew.

He was seated at Mr. Minnelli's side, frantically taking notes on what needed to be fixed.

The girls began their dance. A white flake fell on Bria's nose. It tickled, and she tried to subtly sweep it off before it made her sneeze.

"No flicking flakes!" Marcus bellowed at her.

She was so busy dodging clumps of white confetti that she didn't realize she was *pirouetting* to the left while everyone else was going right.

"You!" Mr. Minnelli barked. "You're going the wrong way!"

"I'm sorry," she apologized. "I was kind of daydreaming."

Marcus stormed down the aisle of seats and up the stairs to the stage. He repositioned Bria stage right.

"Pay attention," he said firmly.

He jotted a note in his binder, which Bria was sure wasn't a compliment.

"He hates me," she whispered to Scarlett.

"Hate is a strong word." Scarlett tried to make her feel better. "Just make sure you follow my lead."

When the waltz started up again, Bria was careful to stay in line and turn in the same direction as the rest of the ballerinas. The girls each held a snowy white branch in their hands as they floated *en pointe* around the stage. The branches reminded Bria of her plant biology experiment. Why wouldn't that little lima bean grow, no matter how much she watered it? How was she supposed to turn in her lab report about chlorophyll if it wouldn't cooperate?

"Glide, glide!" Marcus barked, watching them carefully. "You are supposed to be dancing on ice, not in mud!"

Bria tried her best to look graceful and keep up with the complicated choreography. It was all going smoothly, until she had to wave her branches high above her head and lean to the left.

"Ouch!" shrieked a girl next to her. "Watch where you wave that thing! You could have poked my eye out!"

"I'm so sorry!" Bria said, once again halting the rehearsal. "It was an accident. Really!"

Marcus had seen enough. "You!" he snapped at Bria. "Come over here."

Bria looked at Scarlett and sent her a *telepathic SOS*. She tiptoed over to the corner of the stage where her director was standing.

"Your dancing lacks focus," he told her sternly. "Is there a reason why?"

Bria sighed. "Would you like a list? I have a term paper due on Friday. My math midterm is in a week, and I have no idea how to solve a quadratic equation. Oh! And did I mention I am going to fail science if I don't figure out why my lima beans aren't sprouting. That's it—in a nutshell." She smiled. "No pun intended."

She waited for her director to explode into a Miss Toni-esque tirade. Instead, his face softened. "You know, when I was in middle school, I had a very hard time keeping up with my studies and my dancing," he said quietly.

"You? You had a hard time?" Bria gasped. "You're a legend in ballet."

Marcus cleared his throat. "Yes, well, even

so, my parents put a great deal of pressure on me to excel. I assume you know what I'm talking about."

Bria nodded. "Absolutely! If I don't get at least a B plus, I can't be on the Divas team."

"So here's what I propose," Marcus continued. "When you are here in rehearsal, you focus solely on the task at hand. And when you're at home and in school, you're not allowed to think about *The Nutcracker*."

Bria thought it over. It made sense and seemed so simple—why hadn't she thought of it? She always felt distracted, as if a million ideas were battling to get out of her brain at the same time. If she could just keep them from getting in her way . . .

"And if you need some extra practice time, just let me know," he said. "I think you have a lot of talent. You just have to get your head in the game."

Bria nodded and took her place again in the snowflake line. This time, as she put school out of her mind, her dancing was graceful and flawless. Marcus gave her a thumbs-up, and Mr. Minnelli breathed a sigh of relief.

$$* \quad *$$
$$*$$

The next group to run its scene was the toy soldiers. Hayden and Rochelle took their places in the front row. "Today's the first day we work with our props," Marcus said. He and Miss Andrea distributed wooden rifles.

"Cool," Hayden whispered to Rochelle. He twirled his fake rifle effortlessly in the air and switched it from shoulder to shoulder. Rochelle tried to copy him, but it fell out of her hands and clattered to the floor.

"Butterfingers," Hayden teased, but Rock could feel her cheeks burning. All the boys in the scene laughed and pointed at her. She was happy to be the only girl in the soldier corps—she liked to be the center of attention—but not when she made a stupid, clumsy mistake.

"These prop rifles are probably heavier than the broomsticks we've been using in practice,"

Marcus instructed them. "Handle them with care." He cued the sound crew, and the battle scene music swelled. The group marched in perfect unison around the stage.

"Higher, higher," he said, correcting Rochelle as she struggled to keep the rifle suspended above her head.

When they finished, she was panting. "That thing must weigh at least fifty pounds!"

Hayden held the rifle in one hand as if it were light as a feather. "I'd say about six pounds. You just have weak muscles."

Rochelle raised an eyebrow. "Are you calling me a wimp?"

Hayden chuckled. "Rock, take it easy! I'm kidding around. I'm just saying you are the only girl who's playing a soldier and maybe it's a little tough for you . . ."

Rochelle crossed her arms over her chest. "Because I'm a girl and I can't cut it?" she challenged him. "Is that what you think?"

Hayden shrugged. He didn't know what else

to say. Clearly, he had put his foot in his mouth. "Maybe you just need a lighter rifle?"

Rochelle shoved the prop at Hayden and marched off to her friends in a huff.

Hayden handed both back to Marcus. "I don't get it. Did I say something wrong?"

"I am not one to give advice in the love department," the director insisted. "When I was your age, I had a knack for saying and doing everything wrong."

Hayden suspected he was talking about his breakup with Miss Toni when they were teenagers at American Ballet Company. Rochelle and Scarlett had filled him in on everything.

"What I will tell you is this," Marcus continued. "You want to patch things up before they get in the way of the ballet. And that's not a suggestion. It's an order."

Hayden looked over at Rochelle. He swore he saw steam coming out of her ears. "She's really mad at me. How do I patch things up when she won't even speak to me?"

Marcus demonstrated a graceful *saut de basque* into a bended knee on the stage.

"Okay, I get it," Hayden said. "Beg."

He went over to Rochelle and did the same dance move. He kneeled at Rock's feet and took her hand and kissed it.

"Get up," Rochelle said, tugging on his arm. "This is embarrassing."

"I'm sorry," Hayden apologized. "Please forgive me."

"Aww," Bria said, sighing. "This is so romantic!"

But Rochelle wasn't buying it. "I challenge you to a duel *en pointe*," she told Hayden.

"A what?" he asked, scratching his head.

"You think you're such a big, strong guy. Try walking in my shoes for five minutes!"

She handed him a toe pad and one of her pointe shoes. "You stand on your toes and I'll stand on mine, and we'll see who lasts the longest." She strapped on her left shoe and waited for Hayden to put on his.

"Rock, this is ridiculous. I don't wear toe shoes."

"What's the matter? Too hard for you?" Rochelle taunted him.

"They won't even fit me." Hayden tried to wiggle his way out of it.

"Try mine," Anya offered. "I'm a size nine wide. I have huge feet like my dad."

Hayden slipped his toes into Anya's shoe and laced the ribbon up his ankle.

"This is so silly," he said, limping over to Rochelle. "What is this supposed to prove?"

"That everyone has his or her own strengths and weaknesses," she said. She put on the right shoe and went up in *relevé*. "Do what I do. And Anya, you clock it."

Anya hit the Stopwatch button on her phone. At a mere minute and a half, Hayden broke out into a sweat. "This really hurts, ya know?" he said.

"Does it?" Rochelle said, stifling a yawn. "Doesn't bother me at all. I could do this all day . . ."

Scarlett chuckled. She knew how much Rochelle hated toe shoes as well, but if it meant teaching Hayden a lesson, she wasn't going to give up.

"Ow. Really. I'm losing feeling in my toes!" Hayden grimaced. "Can we please quit it?"

"Are you saying you can't take it? You're just not man enough to stand on your tippy toes as long as I can?"

"Fine!" Hayden exclaimed, dropping back to the soles of his feet and untying the shoes. "These kill. You win. I'm sorry for what I said. I don't think you're a wimp. I think you're incredible."

Rochelle blushed. "Okay, okay. I forgive you. But if you ever insult my muscles again, I am going to use them on you."

Hayden covered his face with his hands. "Please, don't hurt me!"

* * *

With the battle scene and "Waltz of the Snowflakes" under control, that left only one major scene in the Land of Sweets to tackle: Clara and the prince. Olivier took his position.

"Where is Gracie?" Mr. Minnelli called. "We're losing precious time!"

"Go on," Liberty said, giving Gracie a last-minute pep talk. "Remember everything I told you."

Scarlett didn't like the sound of that. "What did you tell her, Liberty?" she asked.

"I just told her that I believed in her, and that she was the star of this ballet. No one should stand in her way."

Gracie shouted back to the choreographer. "In a sec! I have to go freshen up!" Then she skipped off to her dressing room, leaving everyone waiting.

CHAPTER 11

Diva in Training

Miss Andrea found Gracie at her makeup table powdering her nose and applying bubble gum–flavored lip gloss.

"My dressing room is too small," she told Miss Andrea. "I need more room for my stuffed animal collection. Could you maybe move some of the costume racks out into the hall? Or maybe just get me my own dressing room, so I don't have to share with all those people who aren't leads? Oh, and I'd like a big pitcher of pink lemonade before every performance . . ."

Miss Andrea scratched her head. "Um, I'll see

what I can do, Gracie. In the meantime, we need you on the stage. Mr. Minnelli is losing his patience."

A young dancer who was playing a carousel pony walked by the dressing room doorway.

"Hello!" Gracie waved at her. "Would you like my autograph? It's gonna be worth a lot of money one day!"

Miss Andrea ushered her down the hall and back to the wings. But Gracie was far from finished with her list of demands.

"Oh, I also need to make sure that all my second-grade friends get the best seats when they come see me. So if you wouldn't mind asking the people in the front three rows to move . . ."

"Wow, what's that all about?" Anya asked, overhearing Gracie's long list of demands.

"She's become a bigheaded monster!" Bria exclaimed.

"She's become Liberty!" Rochelle chimed in.

"Oh, you flatter me." Liberty smiled, watching her handiwork. "If only I could be in Gracie's ballet shoes."

Gracie finally assumed her position center stage.

"I want to run through your scene with the dolls," Marcus told her.

"Just a sec!" Gracie replied. "I wanna show you something." She turned to face the audience. "Spotlight over here!" she said, waving at the lighting director at the back of the house. "Everybody, watch me!"

She launched into a frantic series of *fouetté* turns, leaps, and cartwheels around the stage. After she landed in a split, she sang out, "Ta-da!"

Mr. Minnelli and Marcus were speechless.

"I think he's gonna kick her out of the show," Bria whispered. "He doesn't look too happy."

"Ya think?" Liberty smiled. She had her fingers crossed behind her back.

"Well, that was . . . energetic," Mr. Minnelli finally said. "But that is not my choreography."

"That isn't even ballet," Marcus added.

"Gracie, I'd like you to please take your place and do what Mr. Marcus tells you to do," Mr. Minnelli said, flustered.

Gracie pouted. It wasn't supposed to go this way. Liberty assured her that as the star, she could add her own "Gracie touch" to the performance.

"But the choreography is boring," Gracie protested.

Scarlett gulped. She was insulting Mr. Minnelli right to his face!

"Boring? How so?" The distinguished choreographer walked down the aisle to the stage to confront Gracie face-to-face.

"It's just . . . well, it doesn't feel like an amusement park. When I go on the rides, I scream my head off and laugh so hard it makes my tummy hurt. It's scarendous!"

Mr. Minnelli scratched his head. "It's what?"

Scarlett stepped forward to translate. "It's scary and stupendous at the same time," she explained. "Gracie-ism."

"Ah, I see," Mr. Minnelli replied, running his fingers through his beard.

"This is not going to end well," Bria said, covering her eyes. "Tell me when it's over!"

"You may have a point, young lady. I do feel the choreography might be a bit dated and in need of some freshening up."

Gracie smiled. "Told ya so."

"But that is my job, not yours. I appreciate your honesty and I will take it into consideration. In the meantime, please take your position."

Gracie stood next to Olivier.

"What were you thinking?" he asked her.

Gracie shrugged. She didn't really have an answer. She knew that if she ever challenged Miss Toni on a dance, she'd be kicked off the Divas so fast it would make her head spin. But Liberty had told her this was different. She was the star and everyone had to answer to her.

"Liberty told me to," she whispered.

"You know what my mom says?" Olivier asked. "If someone told you to stand on your head in a bucket of maple syrup, would you do it?"

Gracie tried to picture it. "It doesn't sound too bad—if you had a ton of chocolate-chip pancakes to go with it."

Olivier sighed. "It means you shouldn't always listen when people tell you to do the wrong things." He pointed to Liberty. "You sure she's your friend?"

Liberty certainly *acted* like a BFF. She paid attention to her and told her how great she was. Scarlett, Anya, Bria, and Rochelle never did that. But then again, it was kind of weird that Liberty suddenly seemed to be on her side.

"I want energy, enthusiasm, wonder," Marcus instructed them. "This is a magical land filled with amusement park rides and cotton candy clouds."

Gracie looked around the stage—she didn't see a single cotton candy in sight. "Where? Where?" she asked.

Marcus gritted his teeth. "All the scenery will be painted and in place for tech rehearsal. We're just going to have to make believe for now."

If there was one thing Gracie was good at, it was making believe.

"K-dokey," she told her director. "I got it."

She flitted around the stage with Olivier, marveling at imaginary marshmallow mountains and gumdrop towers.

"Good," Marcus told them. "Take five."

Liberty skipped over to her. "That was so great, Gracie!" she cooed. "I just have one itsy-bitsy suggestion."

Gracie raised an eyebrow. "What?"

"I think you should tell Mr. Minnelli you need an understudy. All the big stars have them on Broadway."

"They do?" Gracie asked. "How come?"

"In case the star can't go on—which won't happen in your case, of course. But it sounds very official if you have one. I could be yours if you like—that's what friends are for."

"I dunno," Gracie said, shuffling her feet. "I don't think I need one, Liberty."

"Okay, okay, no prob. I just thought you wanted to be treated like a star—not just a little kid like Scarlett and Rochelle think you are."

"I am a star!" Gracie insisted.

Liberty took her by the shoulders and pointed her in Mr. Minnelli's direction. "Then go act like one."

CHAPTER 12

A Brewing Storm

Miss Toni had promised her Divas she'd be there for the final dress rehearsal of *The Nutcracker*, and Scarlett spotted her making her entrance to the playhouse right on time. She was dressed in a long black coat and black earmuffs placed precisely over her perfect ballerina bun. Even on a frigid, blustery day, her teacher looked regal and neat as a pin.

"Hi, Miss Toni," Scarlett said, waving to her. She nudged Anya, who immediately snapped to attention.

"Girls, how's the dress rehearsal going?" Toni asked.

Anya shrugged. "Oh, you know. Just mousin' around."

"I always enjoy watching the mice in *The Nutcracker*," Miss Toni told her.

"Really? Why?" Anya asked.

"Because it's a scene that's fraught with drama and tension," Toni explained. "And it requires a great deal of acting ability to play a mouse."

Anya sighed. "You can't even see my face under the fuzzy head."

"But I can see the emotion your body conveys through dance," Toni explained. "And I will know which mouse you are even without seeing your face—I guarantee it."

Anya suddenly felt a little better about her role. "Well, when you put it that way . . ."

"I will be watching, so I hope you girls make me proud," she said, warning her students. "My reputation is riding on it."

Scarlett nodded. "We won't let you down, Miss Toni," she said. "We've worked really hard, and Marcus says we're doing a great job."

She noticed that her dance coach flinched when she mentioned Marcus's name.

"Yes, well, I'll be in the back, taking notes." She held up her dance journal. "Remember what I always tell you: strength, grace, precision."

* *
*

At the ten-minute call before the curtain rose, Scarlett snuck a peek at the audience from the wings. In the front of the orchestra was Mr. Minnelli, Miss Andrea, and of course, Marcus. She scanned the darkened theater for Miss Toni and saw her way back in the last row—as far away from Marcus as she could get.

"Places! Places! Party Scene dancers to the stage!" the stage manager announced over the backstage speaker.

"That's you, Gracie," Liberty said, shoving her toward the curtain. She raised an eyebrow. "You okay? You don't look so good. Are you coming down with something?" She felt Gracie's forehead.

"I'm okay," Gracie insisted.

"Oh good," Liberty replied. "I wouldn't want you to get all panicky and forget your dance or anything like that."

Gracie gulped. "I . . . I won't."

"K-dokey," Liberty said and grinned at her. "Good luck! Oh, wait! I shouldn't have said that! Good luck is a really bad thing to say to a dancer. Oops!"

Scarlett noticed her sister pacing in the wings. "Gracie," she told her. "I just wanted to say—"

"Oh no!" Gracie shrieked, interrupting her. "Don't say good luck! It's bad luck!"

"I just wanted to say you're going to be amazing," Scarlett said.

Gracie looked worried; her old stage fright seemed to be acting up. "You really think so, Scoot? This star thing is kinda scary."

Scarlett bent down and hugged her little sister. "I don't think you can. I *know* you can! Just be yourself."

Just then, she noticed another figure making

her way through the rows of seats in the orchestra section.

"Is that?" Anya gasped.

"Oh, yes it is!" Rochelle finished her sentence. "What is Mean Justine doing here?"

"She's here to see me," Addison said as she appeared behind them. "Everyone wants to see me. I'm the lead."

"But I'm Clara," Gracie piped up.

Addison waved her hand at Gracie dismissively. "As if you could ever be as good as me."

Gracie gulped. She wished she could think of something to say back to her, something that Liberty had taught her. But all she could do was fight back the tears. Maybe Addison was right. Maybe she had been lying to herself all along.

"You take that back!" Rochelle stood nose-to-nose with Addison. "Or else."

"Or else what? You'll go running to your dumb Divas coach and tell on me? Who cares? Marcus listens to Justine, not to Toni."

She pointed to her City Feet coach in the

audience. She did look very cozy with the *Nut-cracker* director. She was leaning close, whispering something in his ear.

"He obviously listened to her when she twisted his arm into giving you this part," Rochelle added.

"Yeah!" Anya and Bria said in unison, piping up.

None of this appeared to bother Addison. "Say what ya want . . . but I'm the star of *A New Jersey Nutcracker.*"

"There's only one star here, and that's Gracie," Scarlett said, sticking up for her sister. "I've never seen anyone dance it better—not even Gelsey Kirkland."

"Or Barbie!" Bria added. "Just sayin' . . . She had a *Nutcracker* DVD, too."

"Whatevs," Addison tossed back. "We'll see who gets more applause on opening night."

Gracie turned to her teammates. "Thanks, guys, for sticking up for me."

"Are you kidding? What are Divas for?" Anya said, giving her a hug.

"Did you really mean what you said, Scoot?" she asked her sister. "About me being a star?"

Scarlett smiled. "Of course I did. I'm so proud of you, Gracie. And I'm sorry if we were bad sports in the beginning. But I want you to know we all have your back now."

The rest of the girls nodded. "Don't let evil Addison get to you," Rochelle warned her. "She's just jealous. I guess we all were a little."

"That's okay," Gracie said. "I forgive you. And I'm sorry if I was a little show-offy."

"A little?" Anya gasped. "Your head was so big, it was . . ."

Olivier appeared in the wings carrying his giant papier-mâché Nutcracker head under his arm.

"Bigger than that!" Anya said, pointing to the mask.

"I know, I know," Gracie said, sighing. "Liberty just kept telling me I should act like a star. I guess I was acting more like a brat."

"Yeah, demanding only pink M&M's in your dressing room was a bit much," Bria added.

"How about the time you interrupted the rehearsal for an Instagram break so you could post for your fans?" Anya giggled.

"Oh, and how about the time I told Mr. Minnelli he had to make Liberty my understudy," Gracie blurted out.

"Wait! Hold on! You did *what?*" Rochelle asked her.

The girls were suddenly speechless. Of course that had been Liberty's plan all along—to steal the role away from Gracie!

"There is no way you are going to miss a single show," Scarlett told her.

"What if I get sick? Or panic? Or there's a giant tornado that sweeps me away to Oz?" Gracie asked her. "Auntie Em! Uncle Henry!"

Scarlett put her arm around her sister. "We'll make sure you're the one and only Clara. It's like the mailman's motto: 'Neither snow nor rain nor heat nor gloom of night'—or something like that—will keep Gracie from dancing tomorrow night!"

Bria held up her phone. All day, she'd been checking a weather app that was tracking a nor'easter heading toward New Jersey. It was now flashing a red alert. "Um, how about a blizzard?"

CHAPTER 13

Snow Business

After the dress rehearsal, Bria checked the weather app again. "It really doesn't look good," she told her friends. She pointed to a big blue spot on a map of the tristate area. "The blue color is the blizzard approaching. And it's right over New Jersey."

"What if we're snowed in tomorrow? What if no one can get to the theater?" Anya asked.

Miss Toni found them in their dressing room. "The show must go on," she said simply. "I spoke to Mr. Minnelli, and he says that unless the roads are closed or it's too dangerous to drive, he'll open tomorrow night."

"To an empty house?" Scarlett asked. "Anya's

right. What if no one wants to come out in the snow?"

"I promise I will be here," Toni assured them. "So that's one eager audience member you can count on."

"Did you like the dress rehearsal?" Gracie asked her nervously. "Did I do okay?"

Toni smiled. "You did more than okay. Your *arabesques* were glorious. Marcus has really done amazing work with all of you."

"So you don't hate him?" Gracie blurted out.

"Hate him? No, I don't hate him. We're very old friends. Justine, on the other hand . . . she's another story."

* * *

The next morning, Gracie jumped out of bed at 6:00 a.m. and ran to the window. The whole street was blanketed in snow.

"Oh no! The nor'easter is here!" She raced into Scarlett's room and shook her awake. "Scoot! It's a blizzard! It's really bad."

Scarlett peered out the window. It would have been a beautiful winter wonderland if it weren't for the gusts of wind banging the shutters and bending the branches of the trees nearly in half.

"Do you think they'll cancel the show?" Gracie asked her.

"I don't know," Scarlett answered honestly. "It looks like it snowed all night."

Just then, her phone rang. "Are you seeing this?" Rochelle asked her. "Did it have to be today of all days? Why couldn't it have waited until Monday?"

"It's just flurrying now," Scarlett replied optimistically. "Maybe it'll stop."

Her mom appeared at the bedroom door. "The worst is over," she reported. "But there's over a foot of snow on the ground. I'm not sure we're going to be able to dig out of this and get to Paramus."

Gracie tugged on her mom's robe sleeve. "Please, oh pretty please with ketchup on it!" she pleaded.

"It's not up to me, honey," her mom explained.

"The plows have to be able to get through and clear the roads. It's over thirty miles from here to Paramus. I don't know if we'll be able to get to the playhouse."

"We can leave right now!" Gracie suggested. "I'll get my dance bag."

Scarlett stopped her. "Gracie, we can't drive out there right now. It isn't safe!"

"We just have to sit tight," their mom said, "and hope for the best."

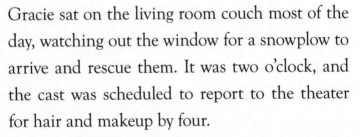

Gracie sat on the living room couch most of the day, watching out the window for a snowplow to arrive and rescue them. It was two o'clock, and the cast was scheduled to report to the theater for hair and makeup by four.

"I could shovel the street in front of the garage," she offered. "Mom could get the car out then."

"What about the rest of the thirty miles to the theater? Are you going to shovel that, too?"

Scarlett asked her. "It's a nice idea, but it's not going to help."

Gracie pouted. "This stinks."

"Why don't you go outside and make a snowman?" her mom suggested. "It's no use waiting around in here. You might as well have some fun."

Gracie pulled on her snow boots and bundled up in her ski jacket and pants. When she took her first step outside on the lawn, she sank in up to her knee.

"It's really deep!" she called to her mom and Scarlett inside. She grabbed a shovel and began scooping together two large balls for the body and head of her snowman.

Scarlett came outside to help and pass the time. "What are you going to name your snowman?" she asked her sister.

"It's not a snowman," Gracie replied. "I'm making a snowcracker."

Scarlett smiled. "I think that's a great idea. Need a hand?"

Together they shaped the balls into rectangles.

"That's way more Nutcracker-like," Scarlett said. They put rocks on his body for buttons and an upside-down pail on his head for a military helmet.

Their mom came outside with a bag of green and red tinsel. "I thought maybe your snowman could use some bling," she said.

"Oooh, I love it!" Gracie said. As she wrapped a red shiny tinsel scarf around her snowcracker's neck, she almost forgot how sad and anxious she was about the storm.

"All we need to do now is his face," Scarlett said. "I think I have a great idea."

She dashed in the house and returned with an armful of food: two lemons for his eyes, a banana for his mouth, and a frozen hot dog for his nose.

"Oh, Scoot! It's awesome!" Gracie said, hugging her. "This is the best snowcracker anyone has ever made."

"I agree," said their mom, who had come outside to see their creation.

"Now you gotta name him," Scarlett told her. "Make it a good one, Gracie."

Gracie scrunched up her nose—which meant she was thinking super hard.

"It's a girl—she's too pretty to be a boy," Gracie finally said. "I'll call her Crackerella."

Scarlett and her mom both applauded.

"And now that Crackerella is all finished, I say we go in and warm up with some hot cocoa," her mom said, ushering the girls in the house. "I can't feel my toes!"

Just as they had gotten out of their wet clothes, the phone rang. Scarlett and Gracie heard their mother talking.

"Yes, we'll do our very best to get there. I understand."

They raced into the kitchen to see who had called. "It was Mr. Minnelli," she told them. "He said the show is still going on."

"Yipperooni!" Gracie jumped up and down. "I knew they wouldn't cancel it."

"But I told him we couldn't promise that we'd

be able to get to the theater," her mom added. "He said not to worry, to just be safe. He has an understudy for Gracie who can go on tonight if we can't get there."

"Liberty!" Gracie and Scarlett shouted at the same time.

"Yes, apparently she stayed overnight at a hotel down the block from the Paramus Playhouse just in case."

Gracie's cheeks flushed. "She is so sneaky! She did this on purpose!"

"Gracie," Scarlett said, trying to calm her down. "She didn't make it snow. She just took advantage of the situation—and you."

Gracie turned to her mom. "We have to get there. Please, there has to be some way."

Her mom shook her head. "I'm so sorry, honey bunny. Unless someone shows up with a sled and a few Siberian huskies, I don't see how. My car just can't make it in this kind of weather."

Scarlett called the rest of the team, and they were all in the same snowed-in situation.

"I know I said I didn't love playing a mouse at first," Anya told her, "but now that we can't get to the theater, I'm really sad. Minnie kinda grew on me."

Hayden and Rochelle were equally disappointed. "All that work, all those hours rehearsing!" Rochelle exclaimed. "And now we're missing our opening night!"

It was 3:45 p.m. and Gracie had just about given up all hope.

"The snow will be cleaned up, and you'll be able to do the show tomorrow night, honey," her mom said, trying to be positive.

"But I'll never have another opening night as Clara." Gracie sniffled. "It won't be the same. Liberty gets to have it, not me." She was about to go up to her room and mope when the doorbell rang. It was Miss Toni and Marcus.

"The highways are pretty clear," Marcus told them. "And Toni called in a favor. We've got a minivan with serious snow tires."

Toni blushed. "A lot of people owe me—this

one just happened to be a former student with a dad who owns a car dealership."

"We've got Olivier, Rochelle, Hayden, Bria, and Anya. Are you girls ready?" Marcus asked.

It took Scarlett and Gracie mere seconds to grab their dance bags and pile into the car with the rest of the Divas.

"Be careful, girls," their mom called after them. "Buckle up."

"Another van is coming for you and the other moms around five thirty," Toni told her. "We wouldn't want anyone to miss opening night."

Just then, Gracie heard the *clank-clank* of chains and spotted the snowplow making its way down her block. "Hooray! The plows are coming! The plows are coming!" She applauded.

As the van pulled out, she whispered in Scarlett's ear, "I bet Liberty is gonna be really shocked to see us!"

CHAPTER 14

We're All in This Together

The van pulled into the parking lot of the Paramus Playhouse just a few minutes after 4:00 p.m. Mr. Minnelli was trying his best to rechoreograph the scenes with fewer dancers.

"Oh thank goodness you're all here!" he said, running and hugging Marcus as he walked in the door. "I couldn't cancel the show, not with the critic from the *Times* coming to review it. Just my luck that he lives in Paramus!" He motioned to the empty stage. "I'm at my wit's end. We're down two mice, a couple of gingerbreads, and a handful of soldiers and snowflakes. No one can make it in all this snow!"

Addison walked through the door. "I made it. I wouldn't miss this for the world," she said with a smirk. Her hair was already done up in a bun and topped with a delicate pearl and rhinestone crown.

"I have my principals, but the corps is a mess," Mr. Minnelli said.

"We can pitch in, Mr. Minnelli," Anya offered. "We can teach each other the choreography and fill in for the missing dancers. We're really fast learners."

Bria nodded. "Miss Toni loves to switch our competition routines at the last minute. I once had to learn a tarantella in ten minutes."

Toni shrugged. "I knew it would come in handy one day."

"All right, if you think you can do it," Marcus said.

"We need more soldiers or the mice are gonna kick our butts," Hayden pointed out.

"I can fill in for a soldier," Marcus offered. "Toni? You game to join me?"

Toni looked stunned. "Me? A soldier in *The*

Nutcracker? I played Snow Queen at ABC, or did you forget?"

"I didn't forget," Marcus replied. "You were spectacular. And I was your Snow King."

Gracie tapped Toni on the arm. "You said there are no small parts, only small dancers," she reminded her.

"You're right," she said. "I wouldn't want any of my team to think I go back on my word."

Liberty stuck her head out of the dressing room to see what all the commotion was about. She was dressed in a white lace-trimmed nightgown and her hair was styled in long, flowing ringlets tied back with a white bow.

"Hey! You look like Clara!" Gracie said, spying her. "Where did you get that costume?"

Liberty was utterly stunned to see Gracie—and the rest of the Divas—filing into the theater. "What are you doing here?" she gasped.

"Um, we're here to put on a ballet," Rochelle replied. "Disappointed?"

Miss Toni gave Liberty a stern look. "You can

change out of that costume this instant," she said. "There's no need for a Clara understudy. Gracie is here."

"There's a big, bad gingerbread costume with your name on it," Rochelle taunted her. "Better go get ready, Lib!"

Liberty fumed. "It's not fair! Why does Gracie get to play Clara?"

Mr. Minnelli held up his hand. "There will be no tantrums, no hard feelings, no diva behavior." He turned to Toni. "Apologies of course to Dance Divas—but you know what I mean."

Toni nodded. "More than ever, we need everyone to pitch in tonight. You'll have to double up on roles and help each other out."

Gracie tapped Mr. Minnelli and whispered something in his ear. "Are you sure?" he asked. "Well, all right."

He faced Liberty. "Gracie suggested that you play a snowflake in addition to a gingerbread."

Liberty's face lit up. "Really? I get to wear one of those beautiful silvery white tutus and a rhinestone tiara? That is so much better than a giant cookie! Thank you, thank you!"

"Thank Gracie," Toni reminded her. "It was her idea."

"Thanks," Liberty said softly. "I'm sorry. I guess I wasn't being a great friend to you."

"You were—in the beginning," Gracie pointed out. "I liked being your friend."

Liberty smiled. "I liked being your friend, too. It's not easy to find someone who loves pink sequins as much as I do. Sorry again for trying to steal Clara away from you."

Marcus glanced at the clock on the back wall of the theater. "I don't want to alarm anyone, but our curtain goes up in less than two hours and no one is in hair, makeup, or costume yet." Everyone stood frozen, not knowing where to run first.

Toni clapped her hands together. "Get moving!" she commanded. Like magic, all the dancers disappeared into their dressing rooms.

"And that," she told Marcus and Mr. Minnelli, "is how it's done."

CHAPTER 15

Curtains Up

The Paramus Playhouse was only about a quarter full—there had been so many cancellations because of the snow. But Gracie was excited to see her mom and the other Diva parents all seated in the front row. Justine was there as well, studying the program and the list of understudies Mr. Minnelli had printed out for the evening.

"I wish we had a full house for opening night," Anya said, peeking through the curtain. "It's like a ghost town out there."

"It doesn't matter," Scarlett assured her. "We're performing for anyone who's watching us—and we have to do the best performance we can." She looked at Gracie and Olivier, who were gearing up to go onstage.

"We're right behind you," she assured them.

"I know," Gracie said. "I'm not scared. I figure if Clara could fight off all those mean mice, I can be just as brave. Right?"

"Right," Anya told her, wiggling her tail at Gracie. "Just try not to hit me too hard when you throw your ballet slipper at my head, will ya?"

Gracie giggled. "I'll try. But my dad says I have a mean pitching arm."

When the curtain rose, the dancers all filed out onstage, pretending to participate in a wonderful Christmas Eve celebration. They danced in lines, with Gracie and Olivier leading them. There was a magician—Clara's uncle Drosselmeyer who was played by Presley in a handlebar mustache and an eye patch—who produced a giant box tied with a bow in the center of the stage. Gracie danced around it, trying to pull off the ribbon and find out what was inside. Finally, the box opened, and Scarlett and Bria *pirouetted* out—as the two wind-up dolls.

"Oh!" Gracie gasped, genuinely surprised to see them in these roles. She giggled as they twirled around her in a doll-like trance, and were finally swept back into the box by Drosselmeyer.

Next up was the battle scene. Miss Toni stood backstage, dressed in a black-and-red military costume with red circles painted on her cheeks.

"You make a very pretty toy soldier," Marcus whispered to her.

Toni half smiled. "Better not let Justine hear you say that."

They marched onstage with Hayden and Rochelle, twirling their rifles expertly as if they were cheerleading batons. Bria and Scarlett only had minutes to change into their mouse suits before Anya pushed them out onstage. They tangled with the soldiers and finally declared surrender. Gracie stood on a bench and cheered as Olivier took the Mouse King's crown and waved it in the air in victory.

A gold coach pulled by carousel horses took Clara and her prince to the amazing Land of Sweets. It was just as magical as Marcus had promised. Gracie couldn't stop staring at the cotton candy clouds floating overhead and the giant Ferris wheel made out of licorice, gumdrops, and lollipops. As she and Olivier sat in the coach watching the action unfold, Addison as the Sugar Plum Fairy flitted around the stage, welcoming them to her domain.

Since the Sugar Plum Fairy's cavalier was stuck in the city because of the blizzard, Hayden had volunteered to play the part.

"I can't watch," Rochelle replied. "This is worse than the time he had to dance with Liberty!"

Addison leaped and twirled around the stage, stepping on Hayden's toes and shoving him out of her way.

"I think she thinks it's a solo not a duet," Anya said. "Rock, you gotta see this! Poor Hayden!"

He struggled to lift Addison in the air as she

squirmed. "Let me go!" she hissed. "You're wrinkling my costume. You're ruining everything!"

So Hayden did just that. He dropped Addison and she landed on the stage with a loud *thud*.

She sat there on her butt, staring out at the audience, as the snowflakes glided down.

"Nice job, Sugar Dumb Fairy," Liberty whispered as she swirled past her. Addison was too humiliated to answer anything back. She ran off the stage crying and rubbing her rear end.

"She asked for it," Hayden explained to Marcus. "She said to let her down."

"Wonderful!" Marcus complained. "Now what? I have no Sugar Plum!"

Rochelle thought fast. "Anya could do it," she said, pulling her friend over. "She knows the part inside, outside, and upside down."

"Fine, fine," Marcus replied. "Go get into the spare costume. You can do the finale."

The audience oohed and aahed over the "Waltz of the Snowflakes." Liberty gracefully glided *en pointe* around the stage, following Bria and

Scarlett's lead. Each of the treats performed a dazzling dance: there were the twisty candy canes, the spicy Red Hots, and the stretchy caramel chews.

When it was time for the gingerbreads to perform, Liberty was first out onstage, leaping through the air and exploding into a breathtaking cartwheel. The rest of the gingerbread dancers waddled in behind her. Their comical routine made the audience roar with laughter—especially when Liberty threw real ginger candies into the audience and pelted Justine in the face with one of them. She ran offstage, panting.

"That was pretty awesome," Scarlett congratulated her. "You stole the show."

Liberty beamed. "I guess this cookie role wasn't so crummy after all."

Next up was the "Arabian Coffee" duet, a mysterious *pas de deux* performed by a couple dressed in matching red-and-gold Middle Eastern costumes. Gracie's eyes widened as she saw Miss Toni and Marcus make their way across the stage as the romantic duo.

"Check it out!" Rochelle pulled Scarlett over to watch from the wings. "Toni and Marcus are killin' it!"

Scarlett was mesmerized. She had never really seen her dance coach perform onstage before. She marveled at her poise and presence; the way she extended her arms and legs into graceful long lines; and how her face captured every emotion the music was trying to convey. "Wow," she said breathlessly. "Just wow."

All the candies came out onstage to perform a grand group number led by the Sugar Plum Fairy. Anya floated onto the stage in a shimmering pink tutu. With a wave of her wand, the Ferris wheel lit up and began to turn. Hayden held her hand as she did a graceful *arabesque* and then bestowed a kiss on Clara's and the prince's foreheads.

In the last scene, Gracie danced around the Christmas tree once again, cradling her nutcracker doll in her arms. Olivier was transformed back into a real boy, and the Land of Sweets faded away with her dreams. She waved good-bye to the Sugar Plum Fairy and the curtain fell.

"I did it! I did it!" she said, as her teammates huddled around her backstage.

"You were an amazing Clara," Liberty said. "I couldn't have done it better myself."

The curtain rose again for bows, and Marcus came out and handed Anya, Olivier, and Gracie bouquets of roses. He had one more bouquet left, which he presented to Miss Toni.

"Thank you—for your wonderful Divas and for saving the day," he told her.

Toni curtsied and kissed him on the cheek. She waved to the audience and was not at all surprised to see that Justine's seat in the front row was now empty.

"I hope we didn't drive her too nuts," she told her girls, with a wink.

CHAPTER 16

Home Sweet Home

After a weekend of wonderful performances, the Divas were sad to see *A New Jersey Nutcracker* end. The area thawed out, and audiences filled the theater to capacity for both the Sunday and Monday shows during the holiday break. The *Times* dance critic called the ballet "a luminous production" and in particular, mentioned "a darling debut by Gracie Borden as Clara, who brought youthful exuberance to the role."

"What's an exuber-dance?" she asked her mom.

"It means you lit up the stage," her mother replied, chuckling. "I'm getting this review framed and putting it up in your room."

Miss Toni gave the girls a mere two days to rest up and recover from the shows. When they came to dance class at four o'clock on Thursday, it was back to business as usual.

"Hang up your toe shoes, Divas," she told her team. "*The Nutcracker* is history, and we're back to competing. Or have you all forgotten what it's like to go head-to-head with Justine and City Feet?"

The girls shook their heads. They hadn't forgotten and they fully expected Addison and her fellow Feet to try and get even for everything that went down during *Nutcracker*.

"We're traveling to Maryland right after the new year for the Sweet Feet competition," Toni explained. "I have the group number all planned out. It's called 'Chip and Dip' and each of you is going to be a giant chocolate chip cookie."

Liberty's jaw fell. "A cookie? Seriously? Wasn't playing a gingerbread dancer torture enough?"

"Well, after you tortured Gracie during *Nutcracker*, I'd say you're getting your just desserts," Rochelle said, teasing her.

"I haven't decided on solos yet," Toni

continued. "But I do know we'll be having a guest join us." The door opened and Olivier walked in, decked out in a red velvet fedora for the holidays.

"Yay! Olivi-yay!" Gracie cheered. "Are you going to be my duet partner?"

"No, you and Liberty are going to be doing a duet," her teacher said without looking up from her clipboard. "I think you actually made a very good team."

Scarlett waited to see if Gracie—or Liberty for that matter—was going to freak.

"K-dokey," Liberty said, winking at Gracie. "Martian twins reunited!"

Miss Toni looked satisfied. "I just want to say how proud I am of all of you," she commented. "And I have a little gift for you for the holidays."

"You're giving us the rest of the week off?" Rochelle asked hopefully.

"No. Nice try. I'm bringing in a guest chore-ographer to work with you while I go visit my family upstate," Toni said. She waved at the studio door and Marcus walked in.

Gracie ran over to hug him. "I thought I'd never see you again!" she said.

"I understand we have a competition to win," Marcus said, taking a seat at the front of the studio.

"Are you sure you're okay about going up against Justine?" Rochelle asked.

Marcus smiled. "Bring it on."

He stood up and had the entire team line up in front of him.

"Okay, gang, let's get crackin'!"

Glossary of Dance Terms

Arabesque: a move where the dancer stands on one leg with the other leg extended behind her at 90 degrees.

Balancé: a three-step motion, usually "down, up, down" (*fondu, relevé, fondu*).

Ballonné: a ball-like or bouncing step. The dancer springs into the air extending one leg to the front, side, or back and lands with the extended leg.

Barre: the wooden bar in the ballet studio that a dancer holds on to with one or both hands to practice/balance.

Coupé: exchanging weight from one leg to another through a closed position.

Changement: it means "changing." A jump in which the feet change positions in the air.

Choreographer: the person who creates the dance, deciding on the steps and order of movements.

Pas de deux: a duet.

Piqué: a movement where the pointed toe of the lifted and extended leg sharply lowers to hit the floor, then immediately bounces up.

Pirouette: a turn on one leg with the other leg behind.

Plié: a bend of the knees with hips, legs, and feet turned out.

Pointe shoes/on pointe: ballet shoes that allow dancers to stand on the tip of their toes; on the tip of the toe.

Prima ballerina assoluta: a rare title given to the greatest female ballet dancers. A very famous ballerina known around the world.

Sauté: a jump using one or two legs.

Tour chaînés/chaînés: a series of quick complete rotation turns on alternating feet moving in a straight line or circle.

Acknowledgments

Many, many thanks to . . .

My beautiful ballerina, Carrie, for always inspiring me with her grace, dedication, and brilliance. Dance like no one is watching!

My husband, Peter—this is what I've been doing at my desk every day! Thanks for putting up with my crazy deadlines. XO

Dances Patrelle for its breathtaking Yorkville *Nutcracker*. Francis, you've given our "Nut kids" and all of NYC an amazing gift. We've loved being a part of it for the past six years and hope for many more to come!

Anne Kelly, Maureen Duke: you take such great care of our kids and teach them to soar! Thanks for your help, always!

Zenmommy and her trio of terrific dancers, Bri, Sophie, and Tristan! Nuggie, Olivier is for you!!!!

Madison Heller and family: we'll miss you in L.A.! Keep dancing and following your dreams!

All the teachers and staff at Ballet Academy East for your love and support—hard to believe it's been ten years of ballet classes for Carrie!!!

My agents Frank Weimann and Katherine Latshaw at Folio, and the wonderful team at Bloomsbury, especially Brett Wright (who makes every revision fun and easy!) and Cindy Loh. Couldn't have done Dance Divas without you.

Sheryl Berk is a proud ballet mom and a *New York Times* bestselling author. She has collaborated with numerous celebrities on their memoirs, including Britney Spears, *Glee*'s Jenna Ushkowitz, and *Shake It Up*'s Zendaya. Her book with Bethany Hamilton, *Soul Surfer*, hit #1 on the *New York Times* bestseller list and became a major motion picture. She is also the author of The Cupcake Club book series with her daughter, Carrie.